WHAT COMES NATURALLY... BEFORE I FORGET

OH HUISHAN

Front & back cover designed by Oh Huishan
Front & back cover royalty-free artwork by Fotolia.com

Title: What Comes Naturally… Before I Forget
Author: Oh Huishan
Editor: Oh Huishan
Publisher: Lulu.com

Printed in United States of America

ISBN: 978-1-257-84686-3

Author official website: www.ohhuishan.com
Business website: www.ohhuishanbooks.com
Author email: huishan@insing.com

For those who need to express themselves and have problems with memory like Dory in the animated movie "Finding Nemo". If you don't remember yourself, will you let others remember you?

Contents

Acknowledgements

I truly appreciate Goddess of Mercy's presence in my life. All of my desires that are for the good of myself have become realized. Thank You, Guan Shi Yin Pu Sa, for being there for me in good and bad times and for guiding me on the right path for myself always!

I would like to thank my mom. With success settling into my life right now, I am learning to become independent, step by step, but I won't forget mom's sacrifices for me. We have our moments as we both get frustrated when caring for each other full time but mom is still the greatest!

I want to thank IMH psychiatrists, psychologists, nurses and medical social workers who have helped and impacted my life in a positive way.

I want to thank anyone who had helped me in anyway.

I would also like to thank all those people who had read about the newspaper article on me and my first book and given me encouragement and kind words.

I want to thank anyone who believes in me.

And lastly, I thank all my readers for their support.

Preface

"What Comes Naturally... Before I Forget" is my 2nd book and it is a collection of prose and short stories from my overwhelmingly emotional self, where "my cup runneth over". My amnesia is pretty mysterious too. Because of my paranoid schizophrenia, I think my "CPU" of a brain is pretty "fragmented" and I wished there were buttons that I could use to "defrag" my brain, truly!

There were many times when just before I woke up from sleep and my consciousness rouses to reality, my brain goes, "Who the heck am I? What is this thing I feel with my senses that is called my body? What is this place I am in that I am waking up to?" Then after a few minutes, sometimes a few seconds, I am jolted back into normality, "Oh! I think I know who I am. I think this is home. Well a body is a body. But what is my name again?"

What comes naturally to me are my emotions and most importantly, my talent for writing. I may not be a Nobel prize winning author and I probably can't compete with English Literature students of high end universities around the world, but I know I can touch my own life by giving my lamentations and idiosyncrasies a structure for ease of cognition through my writings.

I could possibly be touching the lives of other people

around the world through my works and for that I am grateful because I truly love the feeling of being able to inspire.

It really hurts me when I can't write. And there was indeed a time when I could hardly even write my own name properly as my hands trembled, feeling unfamiliar holding a pen. That was during my schizophrenic relapses. It was really bad.

There was constant fear as the voices told me to do their bidding but I finally broke free. Writing is my life. It is probably the only way I can see myself and remember myself. The content that makes my writing helps reflect to me who I am and what I am.

Everything I wrote in this book is a mix of fact and fiction and of different ways of expressing myself. A lot of what I wrote in this book were inspired by different songs be it sad songs, happy songs or just any kind of songs that I liked. I like to flow with my moods in terms of inspiration and that actually helped to give variety to my writings.

I wrote the many pieces of prose in this book in a lyrical way and so don't start getting critical of my grammar and punctuations because it is meant to be like song lyrics. One thing I do promise is that I did my best with the editing of the "Very, very short stories" section.

In the "Psychiatric experiences" prose section, I

expressed my experiences going through schizophrenia. My schizophrenic episodes which had caused fear in me and maybe the people around me when I was severe in my condition should not put off people from trying to understand mental illnesses.

My mental condition makes hallucinations and small tiny fears exaggerated. That is precisely why it is best for me to be on medication. The chemical imbalance in the brain causes the symptoms and when controlled by medication, the images and voices slowly disappear. By expressing my fears, I am hoping that people who do not understand mental illnesses might begin to realize just how exaggerated things seem to be when mental illnesses act out.

I do not make to represent all the people suffering from mental illnesses but I do hope I open windows for people to look into the world of psychiatric experiences, whether it be big or small experiences.

This following prose was written when I was having depression as a teen and I had been hopelessly sad about life. Schizophrenia only struck me in 2004. I found this favourite prose of mine when I cleared up the house with mom in December 2010 to set up a mini office area for me to do my work. Whilst I admired my English standard when I was a teen, I feel so out of touch with writing when I read this.

I wished I could upgrade myself soon in my English and be able to write like I was a teen again. I was only

around 18 years old then and maybe I have more hope in my heart nowadays than in those times. Ironically, I wrote this piece of prose when I was having detention in school. I was depressed about school and I didn't like whatever I was learning for the 'A' Levels. I often refused to do my homework or hand them up. I guess I was a rebel.

No Man's Land by Oh Huishan (2 March 1999)

I strode on in the no man's land,
Feet bare and blistered.
Wearing an armour that weighed a tonne,
A shield in my left hand
And a sword in my right.
The stream of tears ever flowing on my cheeks,
I clenched my teeth tight.
My body was weary
And my heart tired.
The only thing that kept me going was my mind.
Now even that gave up on me
And I fell hard to the barren ground for the first time.
Love, Hope and Courage looked down at me
And shook their heads in unison.
As a breeze blew across this barren land,
They rode with the wind
And left me behind.
Emptiness shrouded me
As I stared into the starless night sky.
An eternity passed before I tensed my sore fingers.
My mind told me to get up but my heart said no.

[It is weird or coincidental maybe? I wrote about Hope and Courage too in a prose called "Loneliness, Hope, Courage and Miracle" in the Psychiatric experiences prose section. That was after I had schizophrenia. I had clean forgotten about this prose I wrote when I was 18.]

My "Very, very short stories" section documents story ideas I have. I don't really have the stamina right now to expand them individually into short novels because of my memory and concentration problems which act out from time to time but I would like to know if you all would like to see any of the short stories become short novels.

Drop me an email to let me know what you like about my very, very short stories and which ones you would like to have as an expanded version. I didn't want to lose any of my ideas and so I guess this book also serves as a portfolio of sorts for my writings.

I do admit that many of my very, very short stories have a morbid or moody theme but I had to write it because that took the depression and fears out of my system like purging does. And I guess I'm a happier woman now. All I can say is thank you for your support!

Now before I forget about my next dosage of medication, my next thought about what next to do, whether I should have gone to buy the Chinese newspapers for mom or even whether I have

switched off the living room lights before I locked the front door to go out and meet up with mom after her work, I want to write something. I want to write down the beautiful thoughts that I sometimes have and share it with everyone. Just before I forget what I was just thinking about...

SECTION I: PROSE

POSITIVE PROSE ON LOVE

A blessing

You looked deep into my eyes,
Wiping away the tears on my face.
You held me really close.
All you said was, "I'm here. I love you."
There on my tongue were words I could not form.
Overwhelming emotions ran through my entire body.
All I could do was cry.
Why did it feel so romantic,
Just for that one moment?
You promised me you would stay.
And I held onto you for the longest time.
All I knew was that you were a blessing in my life.
You held my hand and pulled me out onto the street.
It was raining and we danced,
Heartbeat to heartbeat.
You then said to me,
"I wish this would never end."
All I did was smile,
And you kissed me.
Embracing your face in my hands,
I said, "I never want this to end too."
You smiled,
Crying happy tears.

I'll call

A smile was all I needed.
You really took my breath away.
You said you loved my work.
I blushed and said, "Thank you!"
The next thing I knew,
We were walking down the beach.
We sat down on the bench
And stared at the waves.
You said, "You touched my heart."
I was bewildered.
"What did I do?"
You just grinned and said nothing.
"Maybe we could have coffee together often,
What do you think?"
I didn't even know your name...
I said, "We'll see,
But we can keep in touch."
You nodded silently,
Blushing like a teenage boy.
All I could do was pinch your cheeks.
I said, "You're so adorable!"
I meant to say your abs look great...
I went back to the bookstore
After you gave me your number.
I said I'll call,
And it's a promise.

Love finds you

Looking at the clouds,
I wonder about life and epiphanies.
Have you ever lost something or someone,
So close to you that it hurt?
Did you lose hope?
Or have you given up?
The clouds changed their faces as they floated by.
Nothing ever stays the same anyway.
The pain will heal.
And when the love is over,
Will you look on forward?
Or are you going to stay there,
Staring at the windows?
And when that stranger comes
And stares deep into your eyes,
Will you finally realize?
The one meant for you will come.
You won't need to go searching,
If it is not the right time yet.
Because love finds you.

My heart has finally found its home

Walking down that street,
I was reminiscing the days when we hung out there,
Hand in hand smiling at each other.
I guess it must have been the wrong scene.
Now I have someone else by my side.
He is everything that you weren't
And this is definitely the right scene.
How could I have been so blind?
You were so wrong for me,
And I bet you thought I was so wrong for you.
I won't be retracing the steps we made
And I would be making new footsteps everywhere I go now.
I'd be lying if I said it doesn't hurt anymore.
Even if I have someone new now,
I still feel the pain.
It's not because I still love you,
My heart and soul was trampled by you.
Mistakes you made were always forgivable
And the mistakes that I made were incorrigible.
You're always right,
And I'm always wrong.
That's what you were all about.
I am only human and I have a heart.
I don't deserve to be treated like an unwanted rag doll.
Now I know how to protect myself

And I realized just how precious I am.
I finally know how it feels to be respected.
My heart has finally found its home.

You held my hand

Opening my eyes while I rouse from sleep,
I see you sleeping in my arms.
You were breathing gently,
Feeling safe within my gentle embrace.
All I could do was watch you sleep
And all I felt was love for you.
The more I looked at you,
The more I felt like giving you butterfly kisses,
Loving your handsome manly face.
You move and hold onto me tighter
And I closed my eyes when I felt more of your warmth.
I saw your eyes open
And you smiled at me.
You kissed me and said, "Good morning, sweetheart!"
My heart was pounding so fast it hurt.
You criss crossed our fingers
And you held my hand.
Staring at me,
You said, "I love the way you smile."
I looked away and blushed,
All the while,
Smiling...

Is this how love feels like?

Walking down the sidewalk,
I saw your familiar face as we approached each other.
"I've seen you before..."
You stopped to speak to me.
My heart fluttered when I heard your voice.
Your eyes were sparkling
And you looked at me smiling like daylight.
I smiled nervously and nodded in silence.
"Would you like to go for lunch together?"
You blushed and asked me,
Looking down at your shiny black leather shoes.
I said, "That would be nice."
You walked beside me smiling all the time.
We sat down in the cafe across the street,
Taking turns to blush and smile at each other.
"Is this how love feels like?"
You asked me such a direct question,
I did not know how to answer.
I looked down at my drink,
And then I looked into your eyes again.
"Maybe…"
I giggled as you choked on your cappuccino...

You were by my side

Chasing each other around the beach,
We laughed and frolicked like little winged fairies.
Your smile always made my heart skip a beat.
When you looked into my eyes like that,
My cheeks would blush like a sun kissed doe.
My eyes would sparkle like stars
And your lips would warm mine.
Did you ever know how much you meant to me?
When you played the piano,
Singing songs of love to me,
I could only contain my love by biting my lip.
There is an urge in me to hold you
And never let go.
And when the music notes hit the sky,
All you could see was my joy and happiness
Because you were by my side.

Do you even know?

Would you like to follow me
Into the dark and out into the light?
Would it cause fear in your heart
If I said I could feel you?
Would you groove with me
If I said I loved the way you sing?
All I know is that
I love the way you move.
The way you mesmerize me
With your charming smile,
It makes me want to hold you.
Deep in my heart,
You're the only one.
It doesn't take Shakespeare to know
That I'm in love with you.
But I guess you're just so thick,
'Cause you don't even know.
Do I have to kiss you
To let you understand I love you?
Or it's because you don't feel the way I do?
Someday I will know
But right now,
All I want to do is be next to you.
Thou art love.

NEGATIVE PROSE ON LOVE

Taken

Dusting off his shoulder,
He rearranged his tie.
Smiling like a million bucks,
Gerard looked spiffy.
He walked into his favourite cafe,
Eyeing for the woman he fell for.
Kelly was sitting there sipping her coffee.
She had been hanging out here
Since she started working nearby.
Gerard stood beside Kelly,
Asking if he could sit down with her.
Kelly looked at Gerard and smiled.
Gerard melted that instant.
Kelly then showed him her diamond ring.
"Sorry, I'm taken."
Gerard's heart broke into a million pieces right then.
Kelly continued sipping her coffee.
There were plenty of empty spaces around,
Kelly thought to herself.
Gerard choked on himself whilst his agony reigned.
After composing himself,
He said, "It's alright. Congratulations."
Gerard then walked away,
Leaving traces of his tears on the cafe floor.
He won't be coming here anymore...

Puppy dog eyes

Why does it always have to be
That you're the only one for me?
Songs often sung,
Tears often shed.
Does it matter then
That I make you want to be a better man?
Will I be a better woman for you too?
I can only be who I am,
And you can only be who you are.
Where is your sense of self?
If you keep changing,
Who the heck are you then?
Is it all an act?
Or are you truly in love?
You don't even feel my pain.
If I feel your pain,
Will you feel mine then?
If I truly matter to you,
Will you show it?
Or do I have to wait for a miracle?
Stop your sweet nothings,
And start with real somethings.
Or maybe we're just not meant to be.
Don't do your puppy dog eyes,
This time it won't work.
Now get along then,
Find someone else for yourself.
I've had it,
And I won't stand for it anymore.

All I want to do now is to walk away.
Someday soon my rainbow will come.
And I wish the best for you.
Just don't ever come back to me.

I wished I never met you

I thought you were my soulmate,
The one and only one for me.
The hypnosis I went through...
I saw you and me together,
Life after life.
Was it truly an act of past life retrieval,
Or was it just my pure imagination,
That you and I had loved for so many lifetimes.
We just were never meant for each other
As reality sets in cruelly for us.
Nothing was a match.
It was no wonder it ended in a mess.
We never ended up together in those lives anyway.
But what was it that I felt for you?
Was that my imagination too?
How could something so strong be untrue?
I wished I never met you.
Because then I would never have been left
With so much pain my soul felt destroyed.
If I could live my life over again,
I would cut you out of my life.
We would never cross paths
And we would never have been in love.
So goodbye,
Heartbreaker,
Don't you look back.
And please,
If you ever see me on the streets,
Pretend you never knew me.

'Cause I would never want anyone to know
That I ever knew you.

I return your heart to you

And on that rainy morning,
I thought about a lot of things.
But the one thing which lingered on my mind was you.
Your smile so indelible in my memory
And your eyes were so intense when you looked at me.
Baby, you're the best thing that happened to me.
You cried when I pushed you away.
But can't you see?
I'm not good enough for you.
You have it all going for you
And I am just me.
It breaks my heart,
But I had to do it.
And everyday I wish the best for you,
Hoping that you might meet someone
Who is the perfect match.
Don't cry.
The pain will go away.
It really will.
And meanwhile,
I return your heart to you.

PSYCHIATRIC EXPERIENCES

Mama by my side

Down on my knees,
I beg that the heavens take pity upon me,
For I truly feel so destroyed,
Ever so destroyed.
I have nothing left that is dear to me.
I am truly a failure.
But wait,
What is it that my inner voice says?
"You still have your mom.
She never leaves you in the lurch.
She has been unwavering,
Always by your side."
And so I thank the heavens for letting mom stay by me.
I was so broken and mom picked up the pieces of me
And pieced me back together again.
The unconditional love of a mother towards her child,
No matter what age her child might be,
Is the most beautiful thing on Earth.
Mama kept me safe,
And now that I am better,
I can start helping to keep her safe too.

Fear was all I had

It became darker and darker...
The labyrinth was all I could feel as the lights dimmed.
The walls were hard and cold,
Was it like the dungeons of old?
Panic was rising and I felt my way around the walls.
I could not see my own hands,
I did not know what else to think.
There were hands touching me,
Was it my imagination?
They pulled me here and there.
I could hear their voices telling me,
"You'll never make out of this."
No, it can't be a Hotel California!
Man, was I freaked out!
They came and they left,
Leaving me to vomit and convulse.
It must have been just a nightmare.
I know I will wake up and all this will be gone,
But no, it wasn't a dream.
I fought with all that I had in me.
Eventually they all left and I was left confused.
What just happened?
Now the side effects were all that remained,
I will have to pick up the pieces.
At least I know I am safe now.
The lights brightened up around me,
And I discovered I was not in a labyrinth anymore
But in my own mind,
Screaming...

I wanted to get out

Staring at the ward windows with bars and all,
I wondered when I could leave the psychiatric ward.
I thought to myself,
Will I ever get out?
Fellow patients walking to and fro in patterns,
Praying with hands clasped together.
Well they weren't really praying I guess
But were they?
Screams rang out from them time to time,
I could hear them too,
Those who lived downstairs in the other wards.
I kept talking to the voices unwillingly.
They held me captive and I was obedient.
There were threats to harm me or my parents.
Hey, but wait a minute.
Who's the boss here anyway?
I think that's me...
I just realized the ghosts of my mind were jogging around.
But wait...
Why is a patient hugging my slippers standing next to my bed,
whilst I slept?
I opened my eyes and saw her there,
Smiling like she was possessed.
Someone hugging a bible was tied to the bed along the corridor screaming.
I could smell the smell of meat burning
That came from someone just back from an ECT treatment.

Or was it her hair that was burnt?
In the psychiatric ward,
I was scaring myself
And the fellow patients were scaring me and each other.
All I knew was I was shell shocked.
All I knew was I wanted to get out of there,
As fast as I could.
And when I finally got to leave the ward,
Almost everyone looked at me
And they smiled like they knew.

Death chasing you around

When you walked along the road to nowhere,
Were you excited,
Or were you full of anticipation?
Did it look like it was getting darker?
It seemed like there were a lot of obstacles in your path.
Panic started to set in
And you wondered what the heck you were doing,
Walking along the road that led to nowhere.
Someone drove by and stopped beside you.
You smiled and welcomed the driver as he got out.
Death smiled at you and walked around the car to you.
You screamed and ran as fast as you could.
Death got in the car again and chased after you.
You then fell and rolled down the side of a forest plain.
You began to pray and sincerely willed Death to go away.
Death laughed and suddenly there was silence.
You opened your eyes and found that you were on the
floor,
Just next to your bed,
Realizing you're still in the ward.
A few fellow patients started laughing the same way
Death did,
And they all looked at you
While you ran to the ward door,
Banging for someone to let you out.
The nurses brought you to the little room in the ward
And then injected you with more risperidone.
You then felt more stable
And got back to your hospital bed.

As you fell asleep,
Death creeps away silently,
Leaving a note on your bed saying,
"You were lucky this time."

Fears while I try to sleep

Closing my eyes while I tried to sleep,
My fears came up to haunt me.
"Will I die in my sleep?
Is that how it will all end at the end of the day?"
I feared that I might not wake up the next morning,
Almost every single night.
Then some other nights I ended up wishing I would die sleeping,
Because I felt like I couldn't go on anymore.
Then I heard that little voice in me,
"Hang on! You'll be alright. Believe in that."
Are you sure my little voice?
"I'll be here."
I got some sleeping pills from my psychiatrist
And I slept fine on the nights I took them.
I truly needed to feel like I meant something.
I wished I was useful in life,
Not just a sick bummer.
When I found important things to do,
I stopped having fear of death or the desire to die,
For I meant something to the world.

Would you have lived in vain?

Feeling really frustrated with everything,
I gave a silent scream,
Making my hands into tight fists.
I knew I had made some mistakes
And I needed to forgive myself for the choices I made.
I lived day to day thinking,
Even if no one forgives me,
I still have to be patient with myself.
I feared becoming noticed,
And wanted to live my life in anonymity.
Then I asked myself,
"Do you want to live for yourself,
Or do you want to live by how others want you to live,
According to their wishes?
Would you have lived in vain,
If you were scared of shining like a star?
Are you a robot which does its owner's bidding?
Or are you a human,
Who should live by what is meant for you?"
Staring at the wall,
I squatted down
And rocked myself back and forth.
As I sat down on the floor
And hugged myself,
I cried with uncertainty in my heart.
What would I want others to remember of me,
When I die one day?
With this in mind,
I chose to shine.

Loneliness, Hope, Courage and Miracle

Loneliness can be so heart wrenching.
It is like swimming alone in the middle of the ocean.
You can't see where the land is
And you don't know where to begin or to end.
You scream and no one hears you.
Panic sets in and you hyperventilate.
The helicopters fly by,
Searching for you,
But it seems like they never saw you.
Just when you give up and close your eyes,
And you quit treading water,
Letting yourself sink,
You feel someone pulling you up.
And when you open your eyes,
You see the face of Hope.
Courage lifts your heart out of the depths,
And finally you see land that you can swim to.
Miracle nurses you back to health,
And you finally understand
That you are not alone.

LIFE & RANDOM THOUGHTS

Simplest things in life

Looking out the windows of the bus coach,
The countryside was full of meadows all crisp green
And the sky was all refreshingly blue.
Tears kept running down my cheeks.
I couldn't believe what was happening.
Maybe it was just a very bad dream
That promised never to end.
Then the greenery changed to a concrete jungle,
And I walked along the pavement in my ankle boots.
People were looking and smiling at me.
I guess the simplest things in life
Might just be the best things in the world.
Now I just need to learn to smile again.
I will.
I promise.

Damsel saves man in distress

The wind was blowing on her long tresses.
She laid down on the beach next to the rocky cliff.
He cried his heart out wondering if he should jump.
Ramona turned to her side facing the cliff
And she saw a man wanting to jump from the rocky heights.
Herman and Ramona's eyes met to their own surprise.
Herman stopped crying and his jaw was wide open.
Ramona felt her heart pounding,
Anxious to save this man's life.
Herman's shoes slipped on the rocks
And he dropped into the waters,
Missing a rocky death.
Ramona jumped into the water
And she pulled Herman to the surface of the water.
Herman opened his eyes
And all he saw was Ramona's face and tears.
He managed a smile and a hello
Before he passed out again.

My heart hurts

My heart is in hurt.
It bleeds and it cries.
What do you want,
My heart?
"All I want is for someone to understand."
Spiraling with my inner turmoil,
I am on my knees.
My heart,
Will you please stop hurting?
I can't take it anymore!
My heart just sobs and weirdly enough,
The tears of my heart heals itself.
My heart is on a voyage.
It is searching for that sense of belonging.
My heart,
What are you trying to do?
"I'm just looking for a refuge,
So that you will never be sad again."
But my heart,
It is inevitable to feel sad.
I am only human!
"I know how you feel.
I'm your heart.
And to think of it,
Only you understand me."

I am a schizophrenic

I am a schizophrenic.
People are scared of me
And what I might do.
I am a schizophrenic.
All I want is an answer
But nobody bothers to give me one.
I am a schizophrenic.
When I chase after an answer relentlessly,
I am labeled a possessive
And obsessive stalker.
I am a schizophrenic.
I have not been invited for class reunions
Ever since my friends knew.
I am a schizophrenic.
And maybe that's why people
Hesitate to keep in touch
Because they don't know what to expect.
I am a schizophrenic.
I am prone to suicidal thoughts.
Even the mental health experts in USA say so.
I am a schizophrenic.
All I want is someone to understand me.
I am a schizophrenic.
And all I really want is just a smile
And a pat on my back.

I can be successful

I crouch in a corner of the room,
Fearing the darkness as it set upon me.
It's been almost 7 years
And all I have is fear in my heart.
Success was to me an impossible thing.
I was a total failure,
Maybe even a loser.
I think I need to change my perspective from now on
And come into the possibilities of today and tomorrow.
I need to leave behind the world of impossibilities
And it should all stay in the past as it should.
How will I ever be able to handle
Any good things that happen to me?
I guess I need to learn that I can be successful.
It is not beyond my reach really.
A dose of positivity might just help.
The light shines upon me finally
And maybe there is a world out there waiting for me…
Hello world!

SECTION II : VERY, VERY SHORT STORIES

Does it mean anything, anymore?

"Looking at you, my heart beats faster. Does it mean anything, anymore?" Wei Leong was asking Mei Ling whether she still had feelings for him. Their relationship had come to a standstill and Mei Ling was blowing hot and cold. She still loved Wei Leong though. They had been together for 5 years after all.

Wei Leong had proposed to Mei Ling about a month ago and she had not been acting like herself since then. Wei Leong panicked naturally but it was taking too long and he was near to a nervous breakdown. She had been avoiding him because she was confused about her future. Mei Ling did not know how to face Wei Leong.

Wei Leong was frustrated. Tears ran down his cheeks and dripped off his jaw line. Mei Ling was everything to him. How could she be so cruel? He often imagined a perfect family life together with Mei Ling and he could see kids running around the both of them, laughing together. This was the perfect vision for the rest of his life, a life together with Mei Ling and their kids.

It took 5 years for Wei Leong to have enough courage to get down on one knee and propose to Mei Ling

with a Tiffany's solitaire ring he had saved up for. He felt that their relationship had come to a stage where the only natural thing to do next was to get married. He never expected this kind of reaction from Mei Ling. Or was he the one who had been living in his own delusions? Maybe he never meant that much to Mei Ling in the first place.

Wei Leong kept quiet as he cried. He closed his eyes for a few seconds and took a deep breath. Maybe it's not meant to be and he should just give up and walk away. Wei Leong resigned himself to his cruel fate, turned around and walked away towards the car park.

All Mei Ling did was look at Wei Leong walking away in silence. Mei Ling was not ready to have kids as she was only 22 years old while Wei Leong was 30 years old. Maybe she could bargain with Wei Leong and only have their own children after a few more years. They were still relatively young and had plenty of time.

It was the first time Wei Leong had walked away in silence and Mei Ling's heart went crazy! While she had been pushing him away for a month now, she actually missed him terribly. Mei Ling started walking slowly after Wei Leong and then she ran towards him, crying hot tears of resignation to her own burning heart.

Mei Ling hugged Wei Leong from behind and

sobbed. Wei Leong felt Mei Ling's arms around his waist and heard her sobbing as she whispered a heartfelt apology. He turned around and embraced Mei Ling. His broken heart was whole again and it did somersaults! Mei Ling still loved him!

Mei Ling's heart was hurting so bad. She did not realize just how much she loved and missed Wei Leong until now. Crying still, she said, "Where's my ring?" Wei Leong smiled and took out the ring box from his pocket. Mei Ling held out her hand for Wei Leong to slip on the diamond ring for her.

Wei Leong could hardly contain himself! It meant so much to him to be able to be Mei Ling's man. He held her hand and they walked to his car, crying happy tears. Mei Ling told Wei Leong she wanted to show her parents the diamond ring. All he could do was think about how their wedding day would be like. Everyone was waiting for them to get hitched and Mei Ling's parents loved Wei Leong very much. Mei Ling held Wei Leong's hand in the car and promised she would never break his heart again.

The forests of Okli

The sighs of the ancient trees travelled through the forests, carried by the winds of sorrow. The elven folk shook their heads in disbelief. They had never heard of such sadness in the winds of the forests of Okli. The elven princess Heleza knew what all this meant. The shroud that hides the world of Okligania of the elven folk is becoming thinner and thinner as the humans disregarded the welfare of Mother Earth.

There were many worlds within the world of Mother Earth. Humans might have guessed it but they could never fathom the reality of the different worlds. The answer was very simple. The humans needed to change. Heleza planned to send out an elven army disguised as humans to teach the humans to love Mother Earth. Not all humans were stone hearted and Heleza had to find those nature loving people first so that they could get to work on the rest of the humans.

The elven nymphs dressed in the best gossamer materials of the elven world lined up in the assembly hall of the palace, awaiting the arrival of princess Heleza. The elven soldiers surrounded the palace after they finished their briefing before the elven nymphs went into the hall. They whispered amongst themselves about their worries and doubts on the plan to educate stone hearted humans. Heleza sat

down in her princess throne and the elven nymphs bowed together, welcoming their beloved princess of Okligania.

Tears came flowing down Heleza's cheeks gracefully as she spoke of her sadness about the dying grace of Mother Earth. The winds of sorrow came blowing into the assembly hall to gently remove the sadness in the air and left as quickly as they had arrived. A flock of phoenixes circled the sky above the elven palace. Heleza could hear them and she chanted the spell of shape shifting as they had requested to have the form of humans. They had been sent by their leader to be involved in the mission Heleza was assigning to her elven army.

As these phoenixes landed at the gates of the elven palace, they turned into a group of women with fiery red hair, dressed in the modern way humans dressed. Heleza went out to greet them personally and ushered them into the hall where the elven nymphs were still waiting for Heleza to give further detailed instructions. Phoenixes in Okligania were sacred and for them to take part in the mission meant a lot to the elven folk.

As Heleza walked by the bowing elven army and into the palace hall of elven nymphs where they gathered, she chanted the shape shifting spell again and everyone looked just like normal humans. Heleza told them all to go to the edge of Okligania and prepare to enter the world of humans. The

phoenix women would serve as supervisors and if anyone from the elven army and elven nymphs needed instructions, they were there to advise them.

Heleza collapsed and passed out after the elven army left. She was in deep grief and felt her heart skip a beat when she felt Mother Earth's dying heart. When she awoke from her grief, she looked around her bedroom and suddenly saw a vision of what was to come. There was danger for Okligania and its people but it was going to be alright. The elven priestesses had gathered to pray for Heleza's health and they saw the vision too. Heleza called on the head priestess to discuss about what they had to do to alleviate the situation for their elven army on mission.

Just as Heleza got up from her bed, warriors of the exiled elven rebels came crashing in through the northern borders of Okligania and marched towards Heleza's palace. Now that the elven army was in the human world, Heleza was vulnerable to attacks, they thought. Heleza smiled at the head priestess, Alona. They both knew how powerful they were in their own magic. The rebels underestimated the situation and the power of Heleza...

Turns to dust

Tess looked deep into the eyes of the vampire who tightened his grip on her neck. "Bite me, if you dare. I guarantee you will regret it!" Tess spoke defiantly to him. The vampire went ahead and as his fangs neared the skin on Tess' neck, they turned into dust, as well as his whole being and the dust went with the winds and disappeared into nothingness.

Tess shook her head and dusted herself off. She warned the vampire, it was not like she purposely wanted to "slay" him. She knew there were good vampires out there but not so for this one. Tess was born into a family of vampire slayers and her family was one of the very rare "turns to dust" blessed line of descendants from the Avalonian priestesses who quit living in Avalon and came out to live in mundane England back in the King Arthur days.

Tess received an SMS from her brother, "Are you done yet? I need to get something to eat soon. I'm famished!" Her brother had been keeping a watchful eye nearby but he was not sure whether he could walk over to Tess. The vampire had kidnapped Tess when she got out of the car to look at a broken road sign near the forests.

Matt just sighed and waited in his car. There had never been a single vampire who could remain

whole if they wanted to bite people of his family, even back in Avalon, when his ancestors knew about their effects on vampires. They were trained by the Lady of the Lake as well as the head priestess and Merlin in Avalon.

Tess walked over to the car and got in. Matt was happy he could go and catch a bite now, no pun intended. Tess remembered what their parents told her when she was 4 years old. "Tess, you need to concentrate and blow out the candles on the table." Tess stared at the candles, which were one and a half metres away and focused her intent. The flames died out in an instant. Her family still trained in some magic but their blood lines had inherited automatically the lineage of Avalon magic.

Matt and Tess' ancestors often hid the truth about themselves whilst they lived their day to day life in the nearby village center next to the cloak of invisibility of Avalon. They wanted something more than what Avalon offered: true love.

There had been times when vampires were in large numbers and killed a lot of people in different neighbouring villages. These priestesses had secretly slayed the vampires with their magic from Avalon to save the villagers. Nobody knew of their true identities but the villagers often spoke of a group of women who came in the night and fought with the vampires, slaying them and then disappearing into the night. The vampires turned to dust, according to

what some villagers saw with their own eyes as they were being rescued.

Someone was watching Tess from afar, driving behind Matt's car patiently. Brett had been hiding all this while. He saw Tess whilst Matt's car turned around the corner in the last traffic junction. Brett could not believe his eyes! "Reila!..."

Brett was almost a thousand years old but he looked like he was in his 30s. The only true love he had was Reila and Tess looked just like her. Brett was cursed to live for an indefinite time and his time would be up if he was together again with Reila.

This curse was created by Reila's love rival, Gwenyth, who fell in love with Brett and was rejected by him because he did not feel the same way about her. Reila was the only woman in Brett's heart and she was one of the Avalonian priestesses. Reila was Tess' ancestor. Brett thought to himself, "Could Reila have been reborn again?"

Reila died a violent death. Gwyneth made sure it was hell for Reila as she died. When Brett got to the place he was supposed to meet Reila, he saw her mangled, lifeless body and Gwyneth still wielding a sword at Reila's dead body. Gwyneth had Reila's blood all over herself. She knew Reila was an Avalonian priestess and trained herself in the dark arts to fight her. At least it worked. Gwyneth was able to kill Reila eventually and she had then cursed Brett to a

life of misery.

Matt and Tess had an intuition that someone was watching them. They quickly finished their food at the diner's they had stopped at and got into the car. They then drove around the town centre to try and shake Brett off from following their car. Brett had tears in his eyes and pain in his heart. "Please, Reila. Remember me, even if that means I will die..."

If only you knew

Penny Marge Pickadil closed her eyes. She was losing consciousness as she collapsed to the ground. The vision was too strong for her this time and it caused her deep distress. Penny exclaimed just before she passed out, unable to believe what she had just seen from her vision, "No… It can't be true!"

Matthew picked her up from the ground and carried her to her room. He was crying hard. He never believed that anyone could see the future and he was an atheist. There cannot be any divine at all. Life was just life and it went on only when people were alive. There cannot be anything after someone dies, absolutely not.

How can it be true? Matthew's heart never wavered from what he believed about the afterlife but when he met Penny, something changed. Something about Penny made Matthew want to be a good man, a man who will do anything for his woman and make her feel safe for forever. He did not betray his own heart by starting to believe that there was indeed something more than he could explain out there. Penny took the skeptic out of him and made him a believer.

What Penny saw was a vision that shocked her. She saw her best friend Kathy being murdered by a

police officer she knew. Penny was working in the police force as a forensic psychic medium. She started out giving card readings at a restaurant that had a baby piano and a small table and chairs in one corner for the psychics to give readings.

The psychics worked in the restaurant on a rotating roster schedule. There was a running joke amongst the restaurant staff and the psychics. The psychics were supposed to know their daily roster, right? They were supposed to be psychics, duh! But no, the psychics still had to be notified of their daily working schedules. As Marie, the more famous psychic reader in the restaurant would say, "We're not God. We're just mortal psychics."

Penny looked at Matthew from the doorway. She was having astral projection after she fainted. Matthew was holding her hand and crying. Penny then floated off to the place where Richard murdered Kathy. She saw Kathy's soul lingering nearby her place of death, looking at the buried spot of the knife Richard used on her. Penny kept calling Kathy but it seems as if Kathy could not hear her.

"Penny? Wake up! Please wake up!" Matthew kept calling Penny and her eyes opened. Tears ran down the sides of her face when she woke up and she hugged Matthew hard and sobbed. If Richard knew what Penny knew, her life would be in great danger. Penny sat up in bed whilst Matthew gave her some water and painkillers for the bad headache she had

from passing out.

"Matt, Richard is the one who killed Kathy! I saw what he did and the place he buried the knife. Kathy's soul was there just now! I saw her and I called her but she could not hear me. Matt, what should I do?" Matthew was very worried. He knew Richard must be planning to murder Penny. He never liked Richard. How were they supposed to expose this corrupted cop? Who knows? There might have been other accomplices.
Who can they trust right now?

If Richard was the murderer, did anyone else in the police force help Richard cover up the mess? Matthew used to work for the CIA and he had some contacts he thought might be able to protect them. He called Charlie Hayden, the private investigator who used to be a senior CIA staff. Charlie had retired from CIA as he was getting married at 42 years old. He had then set up the private investigation business with his wife, Angie, who used to be a journalist for the local fashion magazine.

Matthew bit his lower lip in anticipation as he waited for Charlie to pick up the phone. "Hello. How's life, Matthew? I have only ten minutes for you. My wife is getting ready to go out shopping and as usual I would need to tag along and be Mr. Butler."
Matthew explained the situation to Charlie and Charlie assured Matthew that he would help out. He told Matthew to pack up and move together with

Penny to a summer house he owned by the beach. He promised to take care of the rest.

Penny looked out the car window, brooding about what might happen after Charlie takes over. She narrowed her eyes as she felt like her heart was getting stifled. "Do you think someone is following us, Matt?" Matthew looked into the rear view mirror and saw Richard's car right behind them. Richard crashed his car into Matthew's car and sent them crashing into the trees just beside the road on the highway. Penny and Matthew both passed out on impact. Richard was in his police uniform and got out the police car pretending to check on Penny and Matthew while other cars whizzed by the road.

Missing you always

The bus was taking Whitney away from the love of her life. Tears were coming to her eyes but she forced herself not to cry. I have to be brave, she thought to herself. Jeremy was buried just a few days earlier. He had passed away after fighting for his life for the past few years. Jeremy had leukemia and although he had finally found a perfect match with a donor, the marrow transplant was a failure. His body rejected the new marrow and Jeremy's body quickly deteriorated.

Whitney's heart was hurting so badly, her soul felt destroyed. Jeremy was her long time boyfriend for 10 odd years and she had been by his side always. Whitney's family and friends and even Jeremy's family told her to go travel or find a new place to heal herself if where she stayed gave her too much painful memories.

Whitney was not looking at the beautiful scenery that passed by in front of her eyes as the bus drove through the city and into the countryside. She was deep in thought about what next she should do. Whitney had bought a bus coach ticket to the beach and she had brought her luggage along with her. She intended to live there for the next few months to sort herself out before deciding where she should stay permanently.

She arrived at the serviced apartment at the beach and the staff of the residential apartment building came to assist Whitney with her luggage. It was a bit of comfort to Whitney as the staff were very friendly and they always had a smile on their faces. With sunlight, sea breeze and the optimism of the serviced apartments staff, Whitney thought this might just be the thing to help her emotional and mental bearings.

While unpacking her clothes, she felt giddy and kept coughing badly. Whitney covered her mouth as she coughed again and she felt her spittle land on her palm. She went to grab a piece of tissue on the dressing table and wanted to wipe her palm. When she finally took a look at her tissue and her hand, she stood there in deep shock. There was blood all over the tissue. She then realized that it was not normal spittle from a normal cough that landed on her palm. It was blood. Whitney went to the bathroom, still stunned by what she saw, and washed her hand, rinsing her mouth with water.

"What is the address to the nearest hospital? Do you have a map of the area? What bus number should I take then? I need to go see a doctor." Whitney tried to calm herself down and breathed in deeply while calling the reception for help. "Ma'am, we could send you there right now if you need help. We're coming up right now." Whitney freaked out while she waited for the staff to come up and accompany her to the hospital. She kept crying and she trembled all over in

fear. She did not like the taste of blood that still lingered in her mouth. Whitney closed her eyes tightly and shook her head.

The doctor sat down and looked at the x rays on the large computer screen. He shook his head and said, "I'm sorry, you have stage 1 lung cancer, Miss Whitney. You have to be hospitalized right away. We need to put you on chemotherapy and you have to follow through with our medication regiments to fight the cancer cells. We don't want the cancer to spread to anywhere else. It is highly curable since it is only at stage 1 but we don't want to make the mistake of being too complacent about this."

Whitney felt numb, so numb she couldn't feel herself. She passed out and fell onto the floor. Whitney felt a hand holding hers and she heard a man crying, rousing her to wake up from her unconsciousness. She opened her eyes and saw Jeremy there beside her hospital bed. Tears fell down from her cheeks helplessly and she tightened the grip of her hand that Jeremy was holding onto. There was so much she wanted to tell Jeremy and yet she was crying so hard she couldn't utter a single word.

"I want you to fight for your life, baby! Please don't give up just because I'm gone."

"Don't you think it's meant to be? Maybe I'm meant to die and be reunited with you in spirit!" Whitney argued with Jeremy. "How can you be so unfair and

ask me to stay alive when you are cruelly ripped away from my life?" Jeremy hugged Whitney and he couldn't stop crying too because he was as heartbroken as Whitney. The patient in the hospital bed next to Whitney had her radio on and it was playing Mariah Carey's song My All.

I'd give my all to have
Just one more night with you
I'd risk my life to feel
Your body next to mine
'Cause I can't go on
Living in the memory of our song
I'd give my all for your love tonight

Whitney wanted to kiss Jeremy as she missed him so much but he turned his face away and walked away in tears, disappearing as suddenly as he had appeared.

[**Note:** *Mariah Carey wrote and produced the song "My All" with Walter Afanasieff. She wrote the melody and lyrics and the song was released in Mariah Carey's 6th studio album "Butterfly"(1997).]*

The runaway

Adeline adjusted the hood of her warm jacket over her forehead. It was a really cold night and she was so cold, she could not feel her feet, even though it doesn't snow in Melbourne city. She was lying down stretching herself on the bench in between rows of houses on both sides of the large canal. Possums were busy running around on the lower branches of the large tree which stood over Adeline and the bench. She lifted the hood of the jacket slightly to stare into the star filled night sky and she saw many birds flying.

"Wow! Just look at the number of birds flying in the sky! What a sight!" She smiled as she thought to herself. "Wait a minute…" Adeline narrowed her eyes and tried to concentrate on the birds which were flying around in the canopy of the rows of trees along the sides of the canal. "What kind of birds would fly at night in such numbers? Owls, maybe?" One bird flew lower than the others and she caught a glimpse of it before it disappeared, flying higher into the night sky. These birds were actually bats!

Adeline almost passed out. "You're kidding me!" Adeline just could not believe it. How could she be so unlucky? Are these bats even vegetarian? Maybe they drink blood? Oh, how about the size of these bats as they rested and flew around the lower

branches of the nearby trees? Adeline was beginning to regret running away from home. How could she be so stupid? She was trying to calm herself down but she was so scared she wanted to pee. There were no toilets anywhere near her because it was just rows of houses everywhere, surrounding her. She did not want to trouble anyone in the houses by turning up and saying that she just needed to use the toilet. It did not make sense and so she just got up from the bench and relieved herself at the further side of the large tree which was by the side of the bench. She felt like crying for her fear was great and she was shell shocked.

Adeline tried to pretend like nothing was wrong, just in case the bats might react to her hysteria. She laid down on the bench again with her hood over her face. She then noticed the possums stopped running around in the lower branches and kept really quiet. Oh… My… God! Adeline cried quietly. Were the bats coming nearer? Why did the possums stop doing what they were previously doing? Hot tears flowing down Adeline's cheeks quickly turned cold. She blew hot breath on her hands because they were becoming numb.

Adeline suddenly stopped for a short while and laughed hard to herself. She realized that her urine must have had an effect on the possums in the large tree. "I guess I must have marked my territory… And anyway, a human's amount of urine is much more than a single possum's..." Adeline quietly

giggled to herself, fearing this would bring the attention of the bats to herself. "I want to go home…" She sniffled to herself. Adeline trembled and pulled her bag closer to herself. She rummaged through her belongings and took out her small teddy bear. "I love you, my teddy bear, Toto. Don't leave me. I promise I'll be good." She hugged her teddy bear and stayed up all night in fear of the bats which were so far yet so near.

The morning breeze blew on Adeline's cold cheeks and she sat up. She felt so tired but her eyes were wide open, still with the fear that the bats would come and attack her in her sleep. "Lucky I was awake all night! Maybe my urine was helpful even with the bats. Sorry possums!" Adeline kept her teddy bear Toto in her bag of belongings and started walking down the road with much difficulty because she could not feel her feet. She saw some joggers passing by and they said, "Good morning!" to Adeline and she smiled as best as she could at the friendly strangers as her face felt numb from the cold of the night.

Numbers never felt so sexy

Steve was sipping his latte when Yvette walked into the café at the ground floor of the office building which they both worked in. Steve's eyes were wide open and he almost overturned his latte on himself. Yvette was the hot and new accountant at George Smith & Co International on the 8th floor.

People had been talking about her for the past week ever since she started work. She was so slim, willowy and fit and she looked just like Jessica Alba and Megan Fox rolled into one! Steve was in love! Well, Steve's eyes were in love, to be exact. Everyone else's eyes were all in love with Yvette the eye candy. Even the women were checking out Yvette's figure silently.

No wonder men in Steve's office were early for work and left the office much later than the knock off time. They had never been that way before Yvette started work in the same building. Steve was shaking his head at himself and looking down at the floor, stunned by the sight of Yvette. All he could think of in his head was "Wow!".

Unbeknownst to everyone in the café, George Smith was Yvette's father. She just graduated from college and to better prepare her for taking over the business one day soon, Yvette's father arranged for her to start from the bottom as an accountant. Handling the

money was very important, of course, and she needed to gain more experience in the working environment since it was the first time she was working in an office environment.

Yvette picked up her food and coffee and left the café. If a Lamborghini and a McLaren outside the building stopped just next to the ground floor café, no men who were into sports cars would bother looking at them because they were all mesmerized by Yvette. Their eyes were almost popping out of their sockets!

Yvette was used to people gawking at her because she was the college pageant's winning beauty queen and even when she was in her teens, men and boys would try to chase after her. She knew what kind of effect she had on the opposite sex but she was not interested in love. She had her heart broken before and all she wanted to do was excel in her studies and work. All she wanted was to be her father's pride and joy.

Steve was rushing through a report as the deadline was just before work ends at 5pm. Somehow the numbers looked so good in the report nowadays… Numbers started reminding Steve of Yvette. People in his office spoke of how Yvette, being an accountant, made the idea of handling money so sexy. "Numbers never felt so sexy!" Steve thought to himself and had a silly smile on his face.

After Steve knocked off from work, he was just about to enter the lift as the doors opened when he saw Yvette in the lift alone. "Are you going to come into the lift? I'm in a hurry." Yvette was frustrated as she was rushing to meet her elder brother at the lobby and Steve was taking up her time as she held the lift doors open. Steve was so stunned he could not move. He could not believe the luck he had to catch Yvette alone in a lift! He breathed deeply, apologized and quickly entered the lift.

Yvette was quietly looking at Steve in the lift. He reminded her of a crush she had when she was just 16. She smiled to herself and thought, "Looks like this guy works out! His cologne smells so good too…" Steve was going to pass out soon. He was holding onto his only shred of sanity because he had to hold himself back from grabbing Yvette and kissing the daylights out of her. Steve clenched his hands into fists, holding himself steady whilst the lift descended to the first floor lobby area.

What is sanity?

Lauren heard voices telling her to do their bidding. Her neck was stiff and it felt like Alan was holding it tight. He threatened her, telling her that if she did not do what he said, he would break her neck. Lauren was crying and she gritted her teeth, almost locking her jaws really hard.

Alan was not human, he was a vampire. And one that kept giving Lauren visions, hallucinations to be exact. Alan used his willpower to control Lauren and she looked at her right palm. The other vampires that she saw around Alan were scratching at her palm and scratch marks appeared and disappeared.

Something that looked like a banshee and vengeful female spirit rolled into one scratched at Lauren's tummy. Lauren trembled with immense fear and she screamed at the top of her voice while she was sitting on her bed, still unable to move as Alan still held her neck stiffly. She moved her neck slightly and gently, fearful of Alan's hold on her and yet she was anxious to see what happened that was making her tummy so painful. There were fingernail scratch marks all over her tummy that did not hurt the surface of the skin but just slightly underneath. Red trails were everywhere. Lauren almost passed out from the shock!

She was a captive of these supernatural beings… Beings which Lauren wished she never knew. She started feeling pain all over her body and fang marks like that of snakes appeared all over her body, especially on her breasts. The fang marks looked like they were scars which healed over a period of time but they were appearing hard and fast. There were no holes in these fang marks like what would happen if a snake did bite her physically. These beings were making marks on her.

Lauren felt like there was electricity snapping on her skin all over her body. She wanted to pray. She wanted divine intervention to help her get rid of the stronghold these beings had over her. But the truth was that she had lost hope in God. She did not believe in God anymore. How could God let this happen to her? Lauren was not Christian but she believed that there was a God in control of everything before she lost hope in God.

She just gave up and followed instructions given to her by the beings harming her. Suddenly the necklace she wore with a Buddhist pendant snapped and landed on her bed. The beings flew off and left her be in the hallucination. She picked up her broken necklace and held it to her heart, sobbing and trembling, full of deep fear as she examined the marks left on her.

The next day, Lauren's mom called the ambulance service and they whipped her away to the mental

hospital. Lauren was talking to herself and she was kicking and punching into the air, seemingly fighting unseen things. Her mom was worried and truly concerned about Lauren's sanity. While Lauren was sent up to the acute psychiatric female ward from the admissions counter on the first floor, she kept trying to outwit the spirits which possessed her. Their voices gave no peace to her troubled mind.

"Lauren, you are an incarnated angel and your destiny is to help herald the Second Coming of Jesus Christ! You must be responsible for your mission."

"Lauren, don't listen to them. I am sent by Heaven to protect you against these spirits. Follow what I say and I won't kill your mother in her sleep."

"Lauren, I am your higher self. You are the reincarnation of the angel wife of Archangel Michael. This is the truth! You must help Archangel Michael to cast these spirits out!"

"Lauren, go and spit on incense sticks and desecrate them! Incense sticks are hateful things. Never let them into your house!"

Lauren kept using fists to hit her own head as she wanted the voices to stop. She was tired and she wanted to feel normal. She yearned for a peaceful life, a normal life, not a life spent fighting spirits or whatever beings they were. Lauren had gone to many spiritualists and new age healers but none of

them worked. The broken necklace had been the exception. Maybe she should start learning more Buddhist mantras to chant for her wellbeing…

The nurse asked her to strip naked in a toilet cubicle as she wanted to see what kind of self harm had been done. She saw the red trail markings on Lauren's tummy and red spots all over Lauren's breasts. She looked into Lauren's eyes and said nothing. The nurse then handed Lauren the clothes everyone had to wear in the female psychiatric ward that belonged to the mental hospital. "Put on these clothes." The nurse then told Lauren to follow her to her hospital bed. The psychiatric patients in the ward all looked at Lauren when she walked pass them to the nurse station in the middle of the aisle in between beds.

Lauren started crying again. She could feel something growing out of her back. She kept trying to touch her back and she was sure she was growing wings but the nurses told her that it was not true. Lauren screeched, "I'm not an angel! I don't want to be an angel! I don't want to grow wings! Help me! Please help me!" The nurse injected Lauren with risperidone and she finally calmed down. Lauren then felt like she was a newborn baby being rocked gently in a crib and she fell asleep on the hospital bed with the murmurings of other psychiatric patients talking to themselves everywhere in the acute ward.

Lauren was sitting on a lotus flower to her amazement and Buddha was there right in front of

her, sitting on an even larger lotus flower. "Lauren, let go of your past. Just stand still. I will help you but it depends on your karma as well. If you have me in your heart, everything will be alright. I promise you." Lauren smiled for the first time and felt totally safe. She nodded and her eyes opened. The patient next to her bed was holding Lauren's slippers to her chest and standing there by her side, smiling all the time. Lauren jumped out of bed in surprise and grabbed hold of her slippers from the hands of that patient.

Lauren could still hear the voices but she pondered upon her dream of the Buddha. Maybe holding onto the past attracted negativity… Maybe she should just let go and move on with the future but she had to work through the deep set issues in her heart first and that was not going to be easy. But for Buddha, she will try her best. What is sanity anyways? Senseless enmities and mistakes all made life miserable for Lauren. With the last thread of clarity that hung onto the far reaches within Lauren's mind, Lauren tried her best to walk out of her troubled heart. "Wish me luck, Buddha!"

The little cherry blossom

Hazuki smiled at Asuka, her childhood best friend. Asuka held onto Hazuki's hand and assured her that everything was going to be alright. Hazuki was wheelchair bound since she was a child and when Asuka brought her out over the weekend to look at the horses in a farm her grand aunt owned in the countryside, a mishap happened. One of the horses was spooked and galloped in the direction of Hazuki, knocking her out of the wheelchair.

Asuka felt so guilty for bringing Hazuki to the horse farm she was crying inconsolably. Hazuki might have lost her life if the horse did more than just knock her out of the wheelchair! Hazuki squeezed Asuka's hand and said, "Asuka, my dearest friend, it's okay! It wasn't your fault. There was not much damage done at all. I only have a few bruises here and there. Don't blame it on yourself."

Asuka had always adored Hazuki as she was so beautiful and kind, even when they were just kids. Now that both of them were 28 years old, they could probably travel the world together. Asuka wanted to show Hazuki all the places she had been to overseas like USA and Europe, not to mention the rest of Asia.

She had previously worked as an air stewardess and went everywhere she could to travel the world while Hazuki stayed in Japan teaching art and giving violin

lessons to children. The guest house on Hazuki's land inherited from her parents was turned into a small school for students who came to her from all around the world. Hazuki was quite a famous teacher and her quick rapport with students resulted in many successful musicians and artists who had been nurtured by her.

Asuka's grand aunt and some of the staff from the horse farm were outside Hazuki's ward, waiting to go in and see her. They were all concerned about Hazuki's injuries. Right after the doctor made sure the drip was working well, the nurse led them in finally to see Hazuki. Asuka offered to pay for all of Hazuki's medical bills but Hazuki refused. Asuka frowned at her and went to the administrative counter to sign the papers so that when Hazuki was discharged, all the medical bills will be paid by Asuka.

Grand aunt Akiko was very apologetic. They were all very relieved that Hazuki was alright. The doctor said that Hazuki was going to be observed overnight and if everything was smooth, she could be discharged in the afternoon the next day. Asuka pacified grand aunt Akiko and the horse farm staff and then when they left, she went to buy some necessities for Hazuki at the convenient store in the hospital.

Hazuki stared at her legs and she closed her eyes in frustration. Why can't she walk? All she could do

when she saw the horse coming in her direction was try to move the wheels of the wheelchair to the right and even that was not fast enough to get out of the way. If only she could run away from the horse, nothing like this would have ever happened! Her tears of frustration were quickly wiped away as she sat up in the bed because she saw the cherry blossom tree which was just outside the ward window nearby her hospital bed. As the cherry blossoms cascaded down from the tree while the wind gently rocked the branches, it looked so dreamy, it made Hazuki feel like she was in a fantasy world.

"The little cherry blossom, or the little Sakura, was a little tiny flower fairy who lost her way. She had been wishing to travel across the land and visit the flower fairy queen's castle but the black rose fairies blocked her way and cut her with their thorns." Hazuki was writing and illustrating this fairy tale that she was inspired to create. Asuka was so mesmerized by Hazuki's little Sakura sketches in pencil. Asuka had bought a sketchbook and some pencils in case Hazuki was bored and wanted to draw something while she was in the hospital overnight.

"The flower fairy Queen Misaki saw what happened as little Sakura dropped to the ground. The black rose fairies hurt little Sakura's wings and she could not fly anymore. She sobbed as they ganged up on her. Queen Misaki was outraged and put a spell on the black rose fairies. They became stone roses and tears rolled down the stone from the black rose

fairies. Little Sakura stopped crying and looked around to see who had saved her life."

Asuka was anxious to know what was happening next to Little Sakura. Hazuki giggled and said, "Not so fast. Let me think about it first! You'll be first to know. I promise." Asuka grinned and felt better. She was very riled up by what happened to little Sakura. Asuka then went downstairs and picked up a few cherry blossom flowers for Hazuki. Hazuki held them gently in her hands when Asuka passed them to her. They both smiled while looking at her sketches of little Sakura and Queen Misaki.

Asuka brushed her teeth in the toilet the next morning and then helped Hazuki to the wheelchair. Hazuki was looking at her sketches and felt love for the character little Sakura. Asuka made sure they did not forget anything and they took the lift to the car park. The doctor had arranged for Hazuki to be discharged as the laboratory and x ray results were in favor of Hazuki save for a few blue and black bruises.

Hazuki was chatting with Asuka on the way back and Asuka said she got to know a renowned surgeon from USA who was an expert in helping patients with problems in their legs to walk again. Not all of the patients he operated on could walk but most of them did. She had hesitated to mention this to Hazuki as she did not want to make her feel like it was wrong to be in a wheelchair. Hazuki knew

Asuka was not like that but still Asuka did not want to force something on Hazuki just because she felt it was for the good of Hazuki.

Hazuki rubbed her thighs and felt nothing. "Asuka, when can I see that surgeon from USA?"

King of Gustavalia

Timmy turned around when he heard someone calling out his name. Who could it be? "Timmy!" There could not have been anyone around… He was in a desert and travelling alone. Timmy saw something sparkle in the sand. "Timmy! Help me!"

He walked quickly to the sparkling object and swept away the sand. It was a little crystal box. "How did it get here?" Timmy thought to himself. He was hesitant to open the box because there might be bad spells and he did not want to risk it. He started putting it back in the sand when he heard his name called out again, "Timmy! Don't leave me here!"

The tiny crystal sword was anxious for Timmy to release her from her captivity in the sand. Timmy was in a dilemma. He spoke to his own heart silently, seeking its approval. "My heart, should I open this little crystal box to see what is inside? Who exactly is calling out my name time and time again?" Timmy's heart pondered and replied, "Only you can make the decision, Timmy. Look for the sign."

Timmy remembered something and rummaged through his bag and took out a journal. He saw a little symbol on the top of the little crystal box and thought he might have seen it somewhere before. Maybe he could have sketched that down in his journal whilst he started on his own pilgrimage to

find what he had lost.

Flipping through the pages of his journal, his heart grew anxious. Timmy finally found a drawing of the symbol: a crown on a heart. It was one of the treasures of alchemy for a destiny to succeed the throne of Gustavalia, a country in the north where Timmy was born in.

Timmy opened the box slowly and the blinding light that came from it forced Timmy to close his eyes for a few seconds. He tried to open his eyes again and he saw a tiny crystal sword in it that was in the middle of blue sapphires sparkling like drops of water in the big blue ocean just next to Gustavalia! "Hello Timmy. Thank you for saving me. We have work to do. Come now, let me tell you what's first."

The tiny crystal sword sparkled and turned into a mist of blue together with the blue sapphires and flew out of the box, becoming a beautiful woman wearing a dress of blue and she looked like she was the same age as Timmy. Jorene was a princess and she was supposed to marry the king of Gustavalia and become the queen as it was her destiny but the one destined to be king had been lost since he was born.

It was said in the legend that this lost king will only be found when he was alone in the desert by his one true love. There were assassins after Timmy who served the evil uncle of this future king. They had

hunted for him ever since he was born. Timmy never knew who the assassins worked for. Timmy's mother had left him at the faraway village Kaylivak with the alchemists she trusted.

Jorene was under a spell that forbid her to tell Timmy the truth. Timmy was the rightful king of Gustavalia. She had been buried in the desert sand for 300 years and it was no mistake that Timmy found and released her. Only the rightful king could open the little crystal box and have no harm come to him from the spell.

As she looked at Timmy, tears of blue came down her porcelain cheeks which turned into doors that stood in the sand. These were doors they had to go through in order to outsmart the assassins who were getting closer to Timmy. They led to other worlds of existence which no one but the king and his queen could go.

Timmy was exhausted. He had been chased around by people who wanted to kill him everywhere he went. It happened ever since he was born. A kind village couple who had no children took him in when they found him at their doorstep.

Gloria and Jake were alchemists and magicians and they could always hide Timmy so that no one could harm him but when they were murdered whilst Timmy was hiding as a ginger cat in the house, Timmy fled as far as he could from his home. It was

fortunate that he had learnt shape shifting skills from a local shaman who was a family friend of Timmy's foster parents. Henry the shaman had gone missing just the night before Timmy's foster parents were killed.

Jorene knew Timmy's pain and being the handsome young man that he was, she was just content to be around him and protect him. She was born way before Timmy but she was half immortal and time had meant little to her. Jorene's mother was an immortal and her father was a king of Macwulo, a country close to the Orient. It was a land next to the sea of Macwulota which was home to many mermaids and mythical creatures. Jorene knew how to summon help from them but she had no need for that at that moment. She held Timmy's hand and opened a door, walking through to the middle of an iceberg palace, closing the door after them.

ABOUT THE AUTHOR

Oh Huishan (31st October 1981) is a self published author and a stress management coach by training. She is an ex new age junkie turned Christian turned current devoted follower of Goddess of Mercy.

Due to combating with her long term ailment, the mental condition schizophrenia, since being diagnosed in 2004, she decided to use writing as an anchor amidst her chaos and inner turmoil. From barely being able to write her own name to self publishing her debut book "Words That I Can't Say --- A Workbook For Journal Therapy", she has found writing to be very therapeutic.

Her concentration span is improving as the days go by and it was because of the inability to focus for too long that she produced a short debut book. Her 2nd book will also be a short book but will be on pieces of lyrical prose and very, very short stories. Her third project will be a test on her stamina to write a short novel, a step further than a short book but not as long as a typical novel.

Listening to music all day long is a daily must for her. She simply cannot do without music. Sometimes when the psychiatric medication numbs her feelings, she listens to emotional songs and feels like a normal person again. At other times, she just listens to music to imagine about what next she should write. It helps her with

inspiration. Meaningful lyrics of beautiful songs help to inspire her too!

There are times when she has so much to say and because of that sometimes she cannot read books because her mind is overactive and it in turn needs an output through writing. And so she tries to write snippets of stuff here and there until her mind is rested enough to read books.

To find out more about Oh Huishan, visit her official author website www.ohhuishan.com and go to www.ohhuishanbooks.com to check out the list of online retail bookstores her book is being sold in.

www.ingramcontent.com/pod-product-compliance
Ingram Content Group UK Ltd.
Pitfield, Milton Keynes, MK11 3LW, UK
UKHW020328250726
13967UKWH00004B/1911